The Prince knelt to fit the slipper on Cinderella's foot.

STORIES
CHILDREN LOVE

EDITED BY
WATTY PIPER

·NEW·YORK·
·THE·PLATT·&·MUNK·C⁰·INC·

CONTENTS

"Where are you going, Little Red Riding Hood?" asked the Wolf.

LITTLE RED RIDING HOOD

There was once a little maid who had no brothers or sisters. She lived with her father and mother in a pretty little cottage at the edge of the village. At the further end of the wood, which came to the edge of the village, was another pretty cottage, and in it lived her grandmother.

Everybody loved this little girl; her grandmother, perhaps, loved her the most of all and gave her a great many pretty things. Once she gave her a red cloak with a hood, which she always wore afterwards, so people called her Little Red Riding Hood.

One morning Little Red Riding Hood's mother said, "Put on your things and go to see your grandmother. She has been ill. Take this basket for her. I have put in it eggs, butter and cake and other dainties. Now, Red Riding Hood, do not run or you will break the eggs, but you must not waste time on the way." Then kissing her good-bye, she started Red Riding Hood off.

It was a bright and sunny morning. Red Riding Hood was so happy that at first she wanted to dance through the wood. She remembered, however, what her

mother had said about the basket that contained the eggs, so she walked with great care. Soon her steps grew slower and slower; there were so many things to listen to. There was a little brook, there was the song of the birds, and the hum of the bees, and far away there was the sound of her father's axe as he cut the branches from the trees. There were so many things to w a t c h. There were the little squirrels jumping from branch to branch, the rabbits nibbling the tender ferns, and far away the blue smoke from her grandmother's cottage.

All around her grew pretty wild flowers which she loved, and she stopped to pick a bunch for her grandmother, as it seemed to be still very early.

Little Red Riding Hood wandered from the path and was stooping to pick a flower, when from behind her a gruff voice said, "Good morning, Little Red Riding Hood."

Little Red Riding Hood turned around and saw a great big wolf, but as she did not know what a wicked beast the wolf was, she was not afraid and replied, "Good morning, Mr. Wolf."

"What have you in that basket, Little Red Riding Hood?"

"Eggs and butter and cake, Mr. Wolf."

"Where are you going with them, Little Red Riding Hood?"

"I am going to my grandmother, who is ill, Mr. Wolf."

"Where does your grandmother live, Little Red Riding Hood?"

"Along that path, past the wild rose bushes, then through the gate at the end of the wood, Mr. Wolf."

Then Mr. Wolf again said "Good morning" and set off through the wood, and Little Red Riding Hood continued her search for flowers.

Now, thought Mr. Wolf as he trotted along, that little girl will taste very sweet, it is a good plan to keep her to the end. I shall eat up the old grandmother first. On he went and at last reached the porch covered with flowers and knocked at the cottage door.

"Who is there?" called the grandmother.

"Little Red Riding Hood," said the wicked wolf.

"Press the latch, open the door, and walk in," said the grandmother.

The wolf pressed the latch upon the door and walked in where the grandmother lay ill in bed. She was dreadfully frightened, as you can imagine, when she saw the wolf instead of her grandchild. But the wolf did not give her much time to wonder, he was about to spring upon her when she hastened into a clothes-closet that was by the side of her bed, and closed the door. When Mr. Wolf found he had lost a good dinner he put on grandmother's night-cap, which she had dropped in her haste, and then crept under the bedclothes.

In a short while Little Red Rid-

ing Hood reached her grandmother's cottage. She knocked at
the door and walked in, saying,
"Good morning, grandmother, I
have brought you fresh eggs and
butter and cake from mother, and
here is a bunch of flowers I gather-
ered in the wood, and, dear grandmother, I hope you are better." As
she came nearer to the bed she said,
"What big ears you have, grandmother."

"All the better to hear you with,
my dear."

"What big eyes you have, grandmother."

"All the better to see you with, my dear."

"But, grandmother, what a big nose you have."

"All the better to smell with, my dear."

"And what big teeth you have, grandmother."

"All the better to eat you up with, my dear," and with these words the wicked wolf sprang at little Red Riding Hood.

Just at that moment Little Red Riding Hood's father was passing the cottage and heard her scream. He rushed in and with one blow of his axe chopped off Mr. Wolf's head.

Everybody was happy that Little Red Riding Hood and her grandmother had escaped the wolf. Then Little Red Riding Hood's father took her home, and they lived happily ever after.

THE STORY OF PETER PAN

Once upon a time there was a little fairy boy who never grew up. Perhaps that was why he always loved children. Every night he came to a house where lived a little girl named Wendy and her two brothers, John and Michael, with their father and mother and a big dog named Nana, who sometimes acted as a maid for the two boys. And always with this little fairy boy came a tiny dancing light. This was a fairy lady whose name was Tinker Bell.

One night Wendy was awakened by the sound of someone crying. She sat right up in bed and saw this little fairy boy. Not at all afraid, she said, "Little boy, why are you crying?"

The boy sprang to his feet, and taking off his cap, bowed very low.

"What's your name?" he asked.

"Wendy. What's yours?"

"Peter Pan."

"But why were you crying?"

Peter said he came to listen to the lovely stories Wendy's mother told her children so he could retell them to the Lost Boys.

"Who are the Lost Boys?"

"Why, they are the children who fall out of their go-carts when their nurses are not looking.

"If they are not found by their friends within seven days they are sent far away to Never-Land. I'm their captain.

"When I return home the boys will want so much to hear the end of the story about the 'Prince and the Glass Slipper.' I told them as much as I knew and did not want to return until I can tell them the rest, but I must go now," replied Peter.

Wendy begged him to stay with them. "I will tell you lots more," she said, "ever so many more if you will only stay."

"Come, Wendy," cried Peter, struck with a new thought. "You can tell us all the stories there, darn our socks and tuck us in at night. None of us have ever been tucked in. All the boys long for a mother. Oh! Wendy! do come."

"But I cannot fly, and I would not leave John and Michael," replied Wendy.

"I will teach you all to fly," said Peter Pan. "It's as easy as walking on the ground."

So one night he and Tinker Bell and the three children flew away in their pretty nightgowns to the island called Never-Land, where Peter Pan lived.

There were many wonderful things on the island — unknown birds, curious beasts, Indians, Fairies, Mermaids and wolves, and, last but not least, a crocodile who had swallowed a clock and ticked whenever he moved.

Anchored nearby was the "Jolly Roger," a pirate ship, laying in wait to capture six little boys named Nibs, Tootles, the Twins, Slightly, and Curly, who lived on the Island of Never-Land. They lived like moles under the ground, for fear of the Pirates and the wolves. Each one had a staircase made in a tree trunk, so that they could at once run down into the roots of the trees and so to their homes.

They were playing about in a happy way, though they could not think why Peter had been so long gone. Slightly was playing on a pipe, and dancing with a great bird for his partner.

Suddenly the gruff voices of the Pirates were heard. Nibs, who was very brave, slipped away to find out what they meant to do. The others had only just time to get down the stairs in the hollow trees and hide.

The big ugly Pirates came tramping along, their Captain in

the lead. You could not think of a more ugly man than their Captain. His name was James Hook.

Captain Hook wanted to find Peter Pan. It was Peter who, a long time before, in a fight between the Pirates and the Lost Boys, had cut off his left arm and flung it to a crocodile. The crocodile had liked the taste of it so much that he had wanted more ever since. He had wandered from land to land and from sea to sea, licking his lips for the rest of the Captain.

Very lucky it was for Hook that the crocodile had once, by mistake, swallowed an alarm clock, and it ticked so loudly that the Captain could always hear the crocodile coming. While Hook sat down on one of the great forest mushrooms to think how he could hurt Peter Pan and was full of joy over his wicked plans, he heard queer sounds in the distance. Coming nearer and nearer, "Tick, tack, tick, tack, tick, tack."

"The crocodile! the crocodile!" the Captain yelled, and in a moment he was flying for his life.

The Pirates had hardly rushed off to the forest when the Indians crept silently after them. They soon passed far out of sight, and then, one by one, the Lost Boys peeped from their tree trunks.

By and by, seeing that all was quiet, they came out again.

Then Nibs told the Boys how he had seen a lovely white bird.

"It was flying this way," he said; "it looked so tired, and as it flew it cried, 'Poor Wendy.'"

"Are you sure it was a bird?" they asked.

Nibs was quite sure, and almost at once they saw Wendy flying through the trees in her white nightgown. Tinker Bell was by her side, darting at her, and telling the Boys that Peter wanted her shot. Tinker was rather a bad lit-

tle fairy sometimes. She said this because she did not like Wendy.

At once Tootles got his bow and arrow, and shot at the bird, as he thought, and she fell to the ground. Then the Boys saw that she was no bird, but a little girl, and perhaps the very mother whom Peter had said he would bring them.

And just then Peter came flying down with John and Michael, and asked after Wendy.

"She flew this way; haven't you seen her?" he asked.

"Yes," said Tootles, and pointed to her as she lay quite still on the ground.

Peter bent over her and took the arrow and was very angry with Tootles.

At first they thought Wendy was dead, but she was only hurt a little. The arrow had struck a button which Peter had given her as a keepsake.

Soon she was quite well again, but very tired, after her long flight through the air. The boys did not know what to do. They did not like to carry her down into the cave, as it did not seem polite. At last they said they would build a house over her. Only they did not know what kind of a house to build.

Then Wendy sang in her half-sleep the kind of house she wanted:

"I wish I had a darling house
The smallest ever seen,
With funny little walls of red,
And roof of mossy green."

Then they built a house right over her, with branches, leaves and moss, and with lovely make-believe roses trailing over it. And when it was finished they danced around Wendy and shouted, "Please be our Mother!"

"Come in at once," she answered, and they all squeezed in.

There was also a beautiful house underground, where wonderful mushrooms grew at the foot of a Never-Tree. Here the eight boys slept alone in a great big bed. Wendy, of course, lived in that dear little house which they had built her. Every evening Wendy told them stories, and when the stories were done they'd have a dance in their night-clothes, and a pillow fight. In the daytime Peter Pan would take them to the Blue Lagoon, where the Mermaids lived.

One morning Peter and Wendy had a dreadful fright. Captain Hook, of the "Jolly Roger," pur- sued them until they hid on a rock in the ocean. By and by the tide came in and they couldn't get away. So Peter tied Wendy to the tail of a kite which was drifting near, and away she went safely back to the island. Every moment Peter expected to be drowned, but the Never-Bird came by in her floating nest and took him safely to land.

That night, while Wendy was telling pretty stories, the Pirates crept around the little house, fol- lowed by the terrible Crocodile, showing its crunching teeth. At last the dreadful Pirate, Captain

Hook, captured the whole nine children. When Peter Pan came home with Tinker Bell and found the children were gone, he took his trusty dagger and sword and arrived on the ship in the nick of time. Arming the boys, they slew fifteen of the pirate crew. After a thrilling duel with Captain Hook, Peter threw him to the Crocodile, and taking command of the "Jolly Roger," sailed for home, at last leaving the children safe with their father and mother.

Then Peter Pan, who doesn't like houses of bricks, only those made of bending branches and whispering leaves, returned to Never-Land by himself. Every spring he comes back for Wendy, who flies away with him to help tidy up the little house in Never-Land.

DICK WHITTINGTON AND HIS CAT

Once upon a time there lived a poor boy named Dick Whittington, who lost his parents when he was quite young. He strayed about the country for some time, having neither home nor friends. Dick Whittington heard many strange stories from the farmers as they talked with one another on market day in the village. He heard among other things that the streets of London were paved with gold. He longed to go there, so he made up his mind that he would do so and seek his fortune. So he put up his belongings into a bundle, and calling his faithful cat to go with him, he started on the journey. Hour after hour he trudged along until he was worn out. Nobody knows how Dick continued to get food on the road — nor how he could walk so far, for it was a long way—nor what he did at night for a place to lie down and sleep in. However, Dick Whittington reached London safely.

But, alas, once there, he found that he had been deceived. The streets were paved with hard stones covered with mud, and no gold was to be seen. He wandered about friendless and forlorn, for everybody seemed too busy to heed the starving boy. At last he came to the house of a rich merchant and knocked at the door.

The door was opened by the

cook, who seeing a ragged, dirty boy on the step, bade him begone. But at that moment the master of the house, Master Fitzwarren, returned home, and being touched with pity at the boy's miserable condition, ordered the cook to take him in and give him food, adding that he might stay there and do such work for the cook as he was able.

Now, indeed, Dick might have been happy had it not been for the ill-usage of the cook, who knocked him about unmercifully, for she was the most hard-hearted, ill-natured woman. She treated him so badly that the merchant's daughter interfered and tried to protect him, for she felt very sorry for the lonely lad. Yet for all her orders that the boy was to be treated kindly, the cook found many opportunities to torment him.

One day the merchant called his servants together, and told them that he had a ship ready to sail to foreign parts, and that each of them might venture something in her: whatever they sent should pay neither freight nor custom, and they should have fully all it sold for. The merchant's daughter noticed that Dick Whittington was not there, and ordered him to be called.

"But I have nothing to venture," said Dick sadly, "nothing but my faithful cat."

"Fetch thy cat, then, boy," said the merchant, "and send her!" Now, Dick was loth to part with Pussy, for he was fond of the little creature. However, he obeyed his master, and, with tears in his eyes, gave Puss to the captain of the ship.

But after this poor Dick's life became more and more intolerable, for the cook was constantly beating him, and always jeering at him. At last he felt he could endure it no longer, and made up his mind he would run away. He got up one morning very early, and, making up the few things he possessed into a tiny bundle, he slipped unseen out of the house. He trudged as far as a place called Highgate, and there sat down on a stone to rest. And as he so sat, the bells of Bow Church began ringing in the distance, and as they chimed it seemed to Dick that their sounds made a rhyme which ran thus in his ear:—

"Turn again, Whittington,
Thrice Lord Mayor of London."

"Lord Mayor of London," he said to himself. "What would not one endure to be Lord Mayor of London! But if I run away I'll never have a chance! Well, I'll go back again and bear all the cook's pummelling and hard words, rather than miss being Lord Mayor of London." So home he hurried as fast as his legs would carry him, and luckily got into the house before the cook had come down.

While all this was happening

at home, the ship which carried Dick's cat was long beaten with tempestuous waves, and at last was carried by contrary winds to a part of the coast of Barbary unknown to Englishmen, and which was inhabited by Moors. These people received them kindly, and were anxious to see what the strangers had in their ship; so the captain, hoping to trade with them, showed them samples of his goods, and sent also some to the King of the country, who lived about a mile from the sea. He was so well pleased with them that he invited the captain and the factor to come to his palace. Here they were placed, according to the custom of the country, on rich carpets, and, the King and Queen being seated at the upper end of the apartment, dinner was brought in. But as soon as the dishes were put down an immense number of rats and mice rushed out from every side, and, swarming

over the food, devoured it in an instant.

At this the captain and the factor were much amazed, and the latter, turning to the nobles near, asked them if they did not find these vermin very offensive.

"Indeed, we do!" they replied.

"Then why suffer it?" inquired the factor.

"Suffer it!" they exclaimed. "But how are we to prevent it? Our King would give the worth of half his kingdom to know of a remedy."

At this the factor bethought him of Dick's cat, and immediately told the King that he had a little animal on board his ship who would make short work with these disagreeable creatures.

"Go bring this wonderful animal to me," cried the King, "and if what you say as to its powers proves true, I will load your ship with gold and jewels in exchange for her."

"Oh, but I do not know if we can spare her altogether," said the factor, "for then we in the ship shall be overrun with rats and mice as you are. But, however, to oblige your Majesty, I will fetch her for you to see."

"Oh! do, do," exclaimed the Queen, who had listened to all that passed. "I am all impatience to see this wonderful creature."

Off hurried the factor, while another dinner was being prepared, and returned with Puss just as the rats and mice were busy eating that also. Down among them he put her, and she flew round, killing a great number, while the rest scuttled away in dismay at the appearance of this new and unknown foe.

Great was the joy of the King and Queen to see their enemies thus dispersed, and the Queen desired that the cat might be brought near so that she could see her. The factor called out, "Pussy, Pussy, Pussy," and the cat came running to him. Then he presented her to the Queen, who at first was afraid to touch her, upon which the factor stroked the cat, saying "Pussy, Pussy," again. After this the Queen ventured to do so also, and then Pussy curled herself around in the Queen's lap and purred herself to sleep.

The King was so delighted with all this that he bargained with the captain and the factor for the whole of the ship's cargo, and then gave them ten times as much for the cat! So, their business concluded, they took farewell of the King and Queen and the great nobles of the Court, and, hoisting their sails, went with a fair wind to England, and whither, too, we must return.

One morning very early the merchant had gone to his counting-house to arrange his business for the day, when he was surprised by hearing someone tapping at the door.

"Who's there?" he said.

"A friend," was the answer.

"What friend can come at this unseasonable hour?" exclaimed the merchant.

"A real friend is never unseasonable," replied the voice, "and I come to bring you news of your good ship the 'Unicorn.'"

Up jumped the merchant in such joy that he quite forgot his gout, and, opening the door, there stood the captain and the factor with a cabinet of jewels and a bill of lading, for which latter the merchant on running his eye over it, devoutly thanked Heaven for so prosperous a voyage.

"But what have you there?" he asked, seeing the cabinet.

"Why, this is the price of Whittington's cat!" answered the factor, and then he related the story of the rats and mice, and showed the merchant the jewels of immense value which the King of the Moors had given in exchange for puss.

"But, indeed," added the captain, "the treasure is too great for so poor a boy."

"Heaven forbid that I should deprive him of a farthing of it," cried the honest merchant. "Go, fetch the lad at once, that we may tell him of his good fortune."

Now, Dick was busy about his

usual morning work, and when he was summoned was very unwilling to appear in his soiled clothes and dirty hob-nailed shoes in his master's office, but he had to obey, and when at last he entered the room the merchant bade them set a chair for him and begged him to be seated. Dick stared round in astonishment, and then, thinking they were making sport of him, besought his master not to mock a poor simple fellow, but let him go about his business. But the merchant took him by the hand and said kindly, "Indeed, I am in earnest, and I have sent for you to congratulate you on your good fortune, for now has your cat brought you more money than I possess in all the world, and may you live long to enjoy it!"

At last, being shown the jewels, and assured they were all his, Dick fell on his knees and thanked Heaven who had taken such care of a poor boy. Then he entreated his master to accept the treasure, but, the merchant refusing, and his daughter also, he had to content himself with liberally rewarding the captain and factor and all the ship's crew, as well as making presents to all the servants, not even excepting the cross-grained cook.

Now, indeed, did a happy time come to Dick. The merchant invited him to remain in his house till he could procure one for his own; the barber and the tailor were sent for, and when Dick left their hands, with his hair cut and curled and clad in a rich suit, he proved such a handsome fellow that the merchant's daughter straightway fell in love with him, as he indeed had loved her all along for her kindness and compassion to him. The merchant was nothing loth to have so wealthy a son-in-law, and before long the two young people were married. At the ceremony were present both Lord Mayor and Sheriffs, and the eminent merchants of the City.

So the prophecy that Bow Bells rang in the ears of the ragged boy came true. Three times was Richard Whittington made Lord Mayor of London. In the last year of his Mayoralty he had the honor to entertain King Henry V and his Queen on their return from France, and so splendid was the reception given them that the King conferred on him the Order of Knighthood. The King looked round on the magnificence of the banquet, and exclaimed, "Never, surely, did King have such a subject!"

"Nay," replied Whittington, "never surely did subject have such a King!"

So Sir Richard Whittington and his wife lived long and happily, leaving worthy children to succeed them. All his life he showed great charity, and daily fed many poor citizens, remembering how he had wandered, hungry and forlorn, about the streets as a boy. He built a church and college for poor scholars, also a hospital for the sick; so that the memory of Dick Whittington and his cat should ever be held in honor by the citizens of London Town.

Cinderella's Godmother dresses her for the ball.

CINDERELLA

Once upon a time there was a little girl who lived alone with her times lonely. So he married a grand lady who had two daughters

father. Poor child! her own kind mother was dead, and her father, who loved her very dearly, was afraid that his little girl was some- of her own, and who, he thought, would be kind and good to his lit- tle one. But no sooner did the step- mother enter her new home than

she began to show her true character. Her stepdaughter was so much prettier and sweeter than her own children, that she was jealous of her, and gave her all the hard work of the house to do, while the two proud sisters spent their time at pleasant parties and entertainments.

The only pleasure the poor child had was to spend her evenings sitting in the chimney-corner, resting her weary limbs, and for this reason her sisters mockingly nicknamed her "Cinderella." The sisters' fine clothes made Cinderella feel very shabby; but, in her little torn frock and ragged shoes, she was a thousand times more lovely than they.

Now, it chanced that the King's son gave a grand ball, to which he invited all the lords and ladies in the country, and, among the rest, Cinderella's two sisters were asked. How pleased and excited they were when the invitation arrived! For days they could talk of nothing but the clothes they should wear and the grand folk they hoped to meet.

When at last the great day arrived, Cinderella was kept running

about from early to late, decking the sisters, and dressing their hair.

"Don't you wish you were going to the ball?" said one of them.

"Indeed I do," sighed the poor little maid. The sisters burst out laughing. "A pretty spectacle you would be," they said rudely. "Go back to your cinders—they are fit company for rags." Then, stepping carefully into their carriage so that they might not crush their fine clothes, they drove away to the ball.

Cinderella went back to her chimney-corner, and tried not to feel envious, but the tears would gather in the pretty eyes, and trickle down the sorrowful little face.

"What are you crying for, child?" cried a silvery voice.

Cinderella started, and raised her eyes. Who could it be? Then in a moment she knew—it was her fairy Godmother!

"I do so want——" began Cinderella; then her sobs stopped her.

"To go to the ball," finished the Godmother. Cinderella nodded. "Well, stop crying—be a good girl, and you shall go. Run quickly into the garden, and bring the largest pumpkin you can find."

Cinderella could not imagine how a pumpkin could help her to go to the ball, but her only thought was to obey her Godmother. In a few moments she was back again, with a splendid pumpkin. Her Godmother scooped out the inside —one touch of the wand, and the

pumpkin was a golden coach, lined with white satin.

"Now, child, quick—the mouse-trap from the pantry!"

"Here it is, Godmother," said Cinderella breathlessly.

One by one six fat sleek mice passed through the trap-door. As each appeared, a touch of the wand transformed it into a cream-colored horse, fit for a queen.

"Now, Cinderella, can you find a coachman?"

"There is a large grey rat in the rat-trap — would he do, Godmother?"

"Run and fetch him, child, and then I can judge." So Cinderella ran to fetch the rat, and her Godmother said he was just made for a coachman; and I think you would have agreed with her had you seen him a moment later, with his powdered wig and silk stockings.

Six lizards from behind the pumpkin-frame became six footmen in splendid liveries — you would have thought they had been footmen all their lives. Cinderella was so excited that she could scarcely speak.

"Oh! Godmother," she cried, "it is all so lovely!" Then suddenly she thought of her shabby frock.

"There is my white muslin," she said wistfully, "if — do you think——"

But before Cinderella could realize what was happening, her Godmother's wand tapped her lightly on the shoulder, and in place of the shabby frock, there was a gleam of satin, silver, and pearls.

Ah! who can describe a robe made by the fairies? It was white as snow, and as dazzling; round the hem hung a fringe of diamonds, sparkling like dew-drops in the sunshine. The lace about the throat and arms could only have been spun by fairy spiders. Surely it was a dream! Cinderella put her daintily-gloved hand to her throat, and softly touched the pearls that encircled her neck.

"Come, child," said the Godmother, "or you will be late."

As Cinderella moved, the firelight shone upon her dainty shoes.

"They are of diamonds," she said.

"No," answered her Godmother, smiling; "they are better than that —they are of glass, made by the fairies. And now, child, go, and enjoy yourself to your heart's content. Only remember, if you stay at the palace one instant after midnight, your coach and servants will vanish, and you will be the little grey Cinderella once more!"

A few moments later, the coach dashed into the royal courtyard, the door was flung open, and Cinderella alighted. As she walked slowly up the richly-carpeted staircase, there was a murmur of admiration, and the King's son hastened to meet her. "Never," said he to himself, "have I seen anyone so lovely!" He led her into the ballroom, where the King, who was much taken with her sweet face and pretty, modest manners, whispered to the Queen that she must surely be a foreign princess.

The evening passed away in a dream of delight, Cinderella dancing with no one but the handsome young Prince, and being waited on by his own hands at supper-time. The two sisters could not recognize their ragged little sister in the beautiful and graceful lady to whom the Prince paid so much attention, and felt quite pleased and flattered when she addressed a few words to them.

Presently a clock chimed the three-quarters past eleven, and, remembering her Godmother's warning, Cinderella at once took leave of the Prince, and, jumping into her coach, was driven rapidly home. Here she found her Godmother waiting to hear all about the ball. "It was lovely," said Cinderella; "and oh! Godmother, there is to be another to-morrow night, and I should so much like to go to it!"

"Then you shall," replied the kind fairy, and, kissing her god-child tenderly, she vanished. When the sisters returned from the ball they found a sleepy little maiden sitting in the chimney-corner, waiting for them.

"How late you are!" cried Cinderella, yawning. "Are you not very tired?"

"Not in the least," they answered, and then they told her what a delightful ball it had been, and how the loveliest Princess in the world had been there, and had spoken to them, and admired their pretty dresses.

"Who was she?" asked Cinderella slyly.

"That we cannot say," answered the sisters. "She would not tell her name, though the Prince begged her to do so on bended knee."

"Dear sister," said Cinderella, "I, too, should like to see the beautiful Princess. Will you not lend me your old yellow gown, that I may go to the ball to-morrow with you?"

"What!" cried her sister angrily; "lend one of my dresses to a little cinder-maid? Don't talk nonsense, child!"

The next night, the sisters were more particular than ever about their attire, but at last they were dressed, and as soon as their carriage had driven away, the Godmother appeared. Once more she touched her godchild with her wand, and in a moment she was arrayed in a beautiful dress that seemed as though it had been woven of moonbeams and sunshine, so radiantly did it gleam and shimmer. She put her arms around her

Godmother's neck and kissed and thanked her. "Good-bye, dear child; enjoy yourself, but whatever you do, remember to leave the ball before the clock strikes twelve," the Godmother said, and Cinderella promised.

But the hours flew by so happily and so swiftly that Cinderella forgot her promise, until she happened to look at a clock and saw that it was on the stroke of twelve. With a cry of alarm she fled from the room, dropping, in her haste, one of the little glass slippers; but, with the sound of the clock strokes in her ears, she dared not wait to

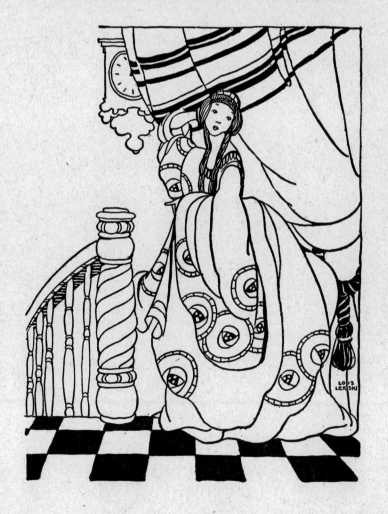

return. When they came in they could speak of nothing but the wonderful things that had happened at the ball.

The beautiful Princess had been there again, they said, but had disappeared just as the clock struck twelve, and though the Prince had searched everywhere for her, he had been unable to find her. "He was quite beside himself with grief," said the elder sister, "for there is no doubt he hoped to make her his bride."

Cinderella listened in silence to all they had to say, and, slipping her hand into her pocket, felt that

pick it up. The Prince hurried after her in alarm, but when he reached the entrance hall, the beautiful Princess had vanished, and there was no one to be seen but a forlorn little beggar-maid creeping away into the darkness.

Poor little Cinderella!—she hurried home through the dark streets, weary, and overwhelmed with shame.

The fire was out when she reached her home, and there was no Godmother waiting to receive her; but she sat down in the chimney-corner to await her sisters'

the one remaining glass slipper was safe, for it was the only thing of all her grand apparel that remained to her.

On the following morning there was a great noise of trumpets and drums, and a procession passed through the town, at the head of which rode the King's son. Behind him came a herald, bearing a velvet cushion, upon which rested a little glass slipper. The herald blew a blast upon the trumpet, and then read a proclamation saying that the King's son would wed any lady in the land who could fit the slipper upon her foot, if she could produce another to match it.

Of course, the sisters tried to squeeze their feet into the slipper, but it was of no use—they were much too large. Then Cinderella shyly begged that she might try. How the sisters laughed with scorn when the Prince knelt to fit the slipper on the cinder-maid's foot; but what was their surprise when it slipped on with the greatest ease, and the next moment Cinderella produced the other from her pocket! Once more she stood in the slippers, and once more the sisters saw before them the lovely Princess who was to be the Prince's bride. For at the touch of the magic shoes, the little grey frock disappeared forever, and in place of it she wore the beautiful robe the fairy Godmother had given to her.

The sisters hung their heads with sorrow and vexation; but kind little Cinderella put her arms around their necks, kissed them, and forgave them for all their unkindness, so that they could not help but love her.

The Prince could not bear to part from her again, so he carried her back to the palace in his grand coach, and they were married that very day. Cinderella's step-sisters were present at the feast, but in the place of honor sat the fairy God-mother.

So the poor little cinder-maid married the Prince, and in time they came to be King and Queen, and lived happily ever after.

SLEEPING BEAUTY

A king and queen once upon a time reigned in a country a great way off, where there were in those days fairies. Now this king and queen had plenty of money, and plenty of fine clothes to wear and plenty of good things to eat and drink, and a coach to ride out in every day; but though they had been married many years, they had no children, and this grieved them very much indeed.

One day as the queen was walking by the side of the river, at the bottom of the garden, she saw a poor little fish that had thrown itself out of the water, and lay gasping and nearly dead on the bank. Then the queen took pity on the little fish, and threw it back again into the river; and before it swam away it lifted its head out of the water and said, "I know what your wish is, and it shall be fulfilled, in return for your kindness to me—you will soon have a daughter."

What the little fish had foretold soon came to pass; and the queen had a little girl, so very beautiful that the king could not cease looking on it for joy, and said he would hold a great feast and make merry,

and show the child to all the land. So he asked his kinsmen, and nobles, and friends, and neighbors. But the queen said, "I will have the fairies also, that they might be kind and good to our little daughter."

Now there were thirteen fairies in the kingdom; but as the king and queen had only twelve golden dishes for them to eat out of, they were forced to leave one of the fairies without asking her. So twelve fairies came, each with a high red cap on her head, and red shoes with high heels on her feet, and a long white wand in her hand: and after the feast was over they gathered round in a ring and gave

all their best gifts to the little princess. One gave her goodness, another beauty, another riches, and so on till she had all that was good in the world.

Just as eleven of them had done blessing her, a great noise was heard in the courtyard, and word was brought that the thirteenth fairy was come, with a black cap on her head, and black shoes on her feet, and a broomstick in her hand; and presently up she came into the dining-room. Now, as she had not been asked to the feast, she was very angry, and scolded the king and queen very much, and set to work to take her revenge. So she cried out, "The king's daughter shall, in her fifteenth year, be wounded by a spindle and fall down dead." Then the twelfth of the friendly fairies, who had not yet given her gift, came forward, and said that the evil wish must be fulfilled, but that she could soften its mischief; so her gift was that the king's daughter, when the spindle wounded her, should not really die, but should only fall asleep for a hundred years.

However, the king hoped still to save his dear child altogether from the threatened evil; so he ordered that all the spindles in the kingdom should be bought up and burnt.

But all the gifts of the first eleven fairies were in the meantime fulfilled; for the princess was so beautiful, and well-behaved, and good, and wise, that every one who knew her loved her.

It happened that, on the very day she was fifteen years old, the king and queen were not at home, and she was left alone in the palace. So she roved about by herself, and looked at all the rooms and chambers, till at last she came to an old tower, to which there was a narrow staircase ending with a little door. In the door there was a golden key, and when she turned it the door sprang open, and there sat an old

lady spinning away very busily. "Why, how now, good mother," said the princess; "what are you doing there?" "Spinning," said the old lady, and nodded her head, humming a tune, while buzz! went the wheel. "How prettily that little thing turns round!" said the princess, and took the spindle and began to try and spin. But scarcely had she touched it, before the fairy's prophecy was fulfilled; the spindle wounded her, and she fell down lifeless on the ground.

However, she was not dead, but had only fallen into a deep sleep; and the king and the queen, who had just come home, and all their court, fell asleep too; and the horses slept in the stables, and the dogs in the court, the pigeons on the house-top, and the very flies slept upon the walls. Even the fire on the hearth left off blazing and went to sleep; the jack stopped, and the spit that was turning about with a goose upon it for the king's dinner stood still; and the cook, who was at that moment pulling the kitchen-boy by the hair to give him a box on the ear for something he had done amiss, let him go, and both fell asleep; the butler, who was slyly tasting the ale, fell asleep with the jug at his lips; and thus everything and everybody stood still and slept soundly.

A large hedge of thorns soon grew round the palace, and every year it became higher and thicker; till at last the old palace was surrounded and hidden, so that not even the roof or the chimneys could be seen. But there went a report through all the land of the beautiful Sleeping Beauty (for so the king's daughter was called): so that, from time to time, several kings' sons came and tried to break through the thicket into the palace. This, however, none of them could ever do; for the thorns and bushes laid hold of them, as it were, with hands; and there they stuck fast and died wretchedly.

After many, many years there came a king's son into that land; and an old man told him the story of the thicket of thorns, and how a beautiful palace stood behind it, and how a wonderful princess, called Sleeping Beauty, lay in it asleep, with all her court. He told, too, how he had heard from his grandfather that many, m a n y princes had come, and had tried to break through the thicket, but that they had all stuck fast in it, and died. Then the young prince said, "All this shall not frighten me; I will go and see this Sleeping Beauty." The old man tried to hinder him, but he was bent upon going.

Now that very day the hundred years were ended; and as the prince came to the thicket he saw nothing but beautiful flowering shrubs, through which he went with ease, and they shut in after him as thick as ever. Then he came at last to the palace, and there in the court lay the dogs asleep; and the horses were standing in the stables; and on the roof sat the pigeons fast asleep, with their heads under their wings. And when he came into the palace, the flies were sleeping on the walls; the spit was standing

still; the butler had the jug of ale to his lips, going to drink a draught; the maid sat with a fowl in her lap ready to be plucked; and the cook in the kitchen was still holding up her hand, as if she was going to beat the boy. Then he went on still farther, and all was so still that he could hear every breath he drew; till at last he came to the old tower, and opened the door of the little room in which Sleeping Beauty was; and there she lay, fast asleep on a couch by the window. She looked so beautiful that he could not take his eyes off her, so he stooped down and gave her a kiss. But the moment he kissed her she

opened her eyes and awoke, and smiled upon him; and they went out together; and soon the king and queen also awoke, and all the court, and gazed on one another with great wonder. And the horses shook themselves, and the dogs jumped up and barked; the pigeons took their heads from under their wings and looked about and flew into the fields; the flies on the walls buzzed again; the fire in the kitchen blazed up; round went the jack, and round went the spit, with the goose for the king's dinner upon it; the butler finished his draught of ale; the maid went on plucking the fowl; and the cook gave the boy the box on his ear.

And then the prince and Sleeping Beauty were married, and the wedding feast was given; and they lived happily together all their lives long.

THE THREE BEARS

In a far-off country there was once a little girl called Goldilocks, because her curly hair shone so very brightly. But she was not so good as she was pretty, for she was often quite naughty, and so restless that she could not be kept quiet at home, and would often run out when she was told not to do so.

One day she started off into a wood, to gather wild flowers and to chase butterflies. She ran here, and she ran there, and went so far, at last, that she found herself in quite a lonely place, and there she saw a snug little house, in which three bears lived; a big bear, a middle-sized bear, and a little bear; but they were not then at home. The biggest of them was called Papa Bear, the next bear in size was called Mamma Bear, and the smallest of the three was their little darling, called Teeny Tiny Bear.

The door and the parlor window being open, Goldilocks peeped in, and soon found the place was empty; so the naughty child made up her mind to go boldly in and look all about the place, little thinking what sort of folks lived there.

Now the three bears had gone out to take a walk, a little while before this. Before going out, Mamma Bear put the nice soup she had made for dinner on a great table in the parlor to cool; as they were hungry, they meant to be back in a short time.

When Goldilocks went into the house, she soon found by the smell that something nice had been cooked, and on going into the par- lor, sure enough she saw three bowls smoking away; the first a very large one, for Papa Bear; the next of middling size, for Mamma Bear; and the smallest of all was Teeny Tiny's bowl; and in each of them was a wooden spoon.

Goldilocks now went to work tasting the soup in each bowl by turns; but she found the soup in the smallest bowl the nicest to her taste.

Goldilocks was now in high glee, and thought to enjoy herself by eating up all the soup in the little bowl. But she was too weary to be standing all the time, so she looked about for a seat.

There were three chairs in the parlor, a very large one for Papa Bear, another of middling size for Mamma Bear, and a nice little chair for Teeny Tiny Bear. The little girl tried them all in turn: she found that the smallest suited her best, and down she sat, and began to eat her soup with great relish.

When Goldilocks had nearly eaten up all poor Tiny's soup, she began to rock herself to and fro in his little chair: she had often been punished for this naughty trick. While she was doing this, out came the rush bottom of the chair, and she and the soup-bowl rolled on the floor. But she did not mind this at all, thinking it was fine fun.

She now thought she would go upstairs, and there we will leave her for the present.

When the three bears came back,

they found that some one had been there while they were out.

"And who has been tasting my soup?" growled Mamma Bear.

"Who has been tasting my soup?" roared out Papa Bear.

Then poor Teeny Tiny Bear cried out. "Somebody has been

tasting my soup, and eaten it all up!"

Then said Papa Bear, fiercely,

Then Teeny Tiny cried pitifully, "Somebody has sat in my chair, and broken it!"

"Who has been using my chair?" Mamma Bear, too, said, "Who has been sitting on my chair?"

In the room upstairs there were three beds: the largest was Papa Bear's bed; the next was Mamma

Bear's bed; and the smallest of the three beds was Teeny Tiny's bed.

Goldilocks tried them all, but she found the little one the most comfortable; and as she was very sleepy, she crept into it, and fell fast asleep.

The three bears, thinking that somebody was in the house, came upstairs to look, and found their beds had been disturbed, and they all, in angry voices, asked who had dared to do it.

Goldilocks did not hear the gruff voices of Papa and Mamma Bear, but the sharp squeak of Teeny Tiny's voice aroused her from her slumber.

"Somebody has been lying on my bed!" cried he; and in a moment after he added, "And here she is!" looking at the same time as fierce as a little bear who had lost his dinner could do.

The little girl was now almost frightened to death, especially when she saw at the other end of the room two larger bears, in a terrible rage. Luckily for her, there was an open window close to Tiny's bed, and seeing this, she jumped out of bed in a moment, and then took a spring, and escaped out of the window.

The three bears came to the open window, and stared wildly at her, so she got up, and ran as fast as she could until she got safe home again.

Here she was properly punished for her bad behavior, besides the great fright she suffered from the savage looks and angry growling of the three bears.

PUSS IN BOOTS

ONCE upon a time there was a miller, who was so poor that at his death he had nothing to leave to his three children but his mill, his ass, and his cat. The eldest son took the mill, and the second the ass, so there was nothing left for poor Jack but to take Puss.

Jack could not help thinking that he had been treated shabbily. "My brothers will be able to earn an honest livlihood," he sighed, "but as for me, though Puss may feed himself by catching mice, I shall certainly die of hunger."

The cat, who had overheard his young master, jumped upon his shoulder, and, rubbing himself gently against his cheek, began to speak. "Dear master," said he, "do not grieve. I am not as useless as you think me, and will undertake to make your fortune for you, if only you will buy me a pair of boots, and give me that old bag."

Now, Jack had very little money to spare, but, knowing Puss to be a faithful old friend, he made up his mind to trust him, and so spent all he possessed upon a smart pair of boots made of buff-colored leather. They fitted per-

fectly, so Puss put them on, took the old bag which his master gave him, and trotted off to a neighboring warren in which he knew there was a great number of rabbits.

Having put some bran and fresh parsley into the bag, he laid it upon the ground, hid himself, and waited. Presently two foolish little rabbits, sniffing the food, ran straight into the bag, when the clever cat drew the strings and caught them.

Then, slinging the bag over his shoulder, he hastened off to the palace, where he asked to speak to the King. Having been shown into the royal presence, he bowed and said:

"Sire, my Lord the Marquis of Carabas has commanded me to present these rabbits to your Majesty, with his respects."

The monarch having desired his thanks to be given to the Marquis (who, as you will guess, was really our poor Jack), then ordered his head cook to dress the rabbits for dinner, and he and his daughter partook of them with great enjoyment.

Day by day Puss brought home stores of good food, so that he and his master lived in plenty, and besides that, he did not fail to keep the King and his courtiers well supplied with game.

Sometimes he would lay a brace

of partridges at the royal feet, sometimes a fine large hare, but whatever it was, it always came with the same message: "From my Lord the Marquis of Carabas"; so that everyone at Court was talking of this strange nobleman, whom no one had ever seen, but

who sent such generous presents to his Majesty.

At length Puss decided that it was time for his master to be introduced at Court. So one day he persuaded him to go and bathe in a river near, having heard that the King would soon pass that way.

Jack stood shivering up to his neck in water, wondering what was to happen next, when suddenly the King's carriage appeared in sight. At once Puss began to call out as loudly as he could:

"Help, help! My Lord the Marquis of Carabas is drowning!"

The King put his head out of the carriage window and, recognizing the cat, ordered his attendants to go to the assistance of the Marquis. While Jack was being taken out of the water, Puss ran to the King and told him that some robbers had run off with his master's clothes while he was bathing, the truth of the matter being that the cunning cat had hidden them under a stone.

On hearing this story the King instantly despatched one of his grooms to fetch a handsome suit of purple and gold from the royal wardrobe, and arrayed in this, Jack, who was a fine, handsome fellow, looked so well that no one for a moment supposed but that he was some noble foreign lord.

The King and his daughter were so pleased with his appearance that they invited him into their carriage. At first Jack hesitated, for he felt a little shy about sitting next to a Princess, but she smiled at him so sweetly, and was so kind and gentle, that he soon forgot his fears and fell in love with her then and there.

As soon as Puss had seen his

master seated in the royal carriage, he whispered directions to the coachman, and then ran on ahead as fast as he could trot, until he came to a field of corn, where the reapers were busy.

"Reapers," said he fiercely, "the King will shortly pass this way. If he should ask you to whom this field belongs, remember that you say, 'To the Marquis of Carabas.' If you dare to disobey me, I will have you all chopped up as fine as mincemeat." The reapers were so afraid the cat would keep his word that they promised to obey. Puss then ran on and told all the other laborers whom he met to give the same answer, threatening them with terrible punishments if they disobeyed.

Now, the King was in a very good humor, for the day was fine, and he found the Marquis a very pleasant companion, so he told the coachman to drive slowly, in order that he might admire the beautiful country. "What a fine field of wheat!" he said presently. "To whom does it belong?" Then the men answered as they had been told: "To our Lord the Marquis of Carabas." Next they met a herd of cattle, and again to the King's question, "To whom do they belong?" they were told, "To the Marquis of Carabas." And it was the same with everything they passed.

The Marquis listened with the greatest astonishment, and thought what a very wonderful cat his dear Puss was; and the King was delighted to find that his new friend was as wealthy as he was charming.

Meanwhile Puss, who was well in advance of the Royal party, had arrived at a stately castle, which belonged to a cruel Ogre, the richest ever known, for all the lands the King had admired so much belonged to him. Puss knocked at the door and asked to

see the Ogre, who received him quite civilly, for he had never seen a cat in boots before.

So he and Puss were soon chatting away together.

"I once heard," Puss said at last, "that you had the power of changing yourself into any kind of an animal you chose—a lion or an elephant, for instance."

"Well, so I can," replied the Ogre.

"Dear me! how much I should like to see you do it now," said Puss sweetly.

The Ogre promised to transform himself into any animal Puss might mention.

"Oh! I will leave the choice to you," said the cat politely.

Immediately there appeared, where the Ogre had been seated, an enormous roaring lion.

Puss was very much frightened, and jumping out of the window, managed to scramble on to the roof.

There he sat until the Ogre changed himself into his natural form.

Then Puss ventured back into the room, and began to compliment the Ogre on his cleverness.

"Of course, it was all very wonderful," he said, "but it would be

more wonderful if you could transform yourself into some little creature, such as a mouse. That, I suppose, would be quite impossible?"

"Not at all," said the vain Ogre; "one is quite as easy for me as the other, as I will show you." And in a moment a little mouse was frisking about the floor, and the Ogre had vanished.

"Now or never," said Puss, and with a spring he seized the mouse and gobbled it up.

At that moment all the gentlemen and ladies, whom the wicked Ogre had held in his castle under a spell, became disenchanted. They were so grateful to their deliverer that they readily agreed to enter into the service of the Marquis of Carabas when Puss asked them.

So now the cat had a splendid castle, which he knew to be full of treasures. He ordered a magnificent feast to be prepared, and took up his station at the castle gates to welcome his master and the royal party.

As soon as the castle appeared in sight, the King inquired whose it was, "for," said he, "I have never seen a finer."

Then Puss, bowing low, threw open the castle gates, and cried:

"May it please your Majesty to alight and enter the home of the Marquis of Carabas."

Puss then helped his Majesty to alight, and conducted him into the castle. Jack, or the Marquis as he was now called, gave his hand to the young Princess, and led her to the banquet. Long and merrily they feasted, and when at length the guests rose to depart, the King embraced the Marquis, and called him his dear son; and the Princess blushed so shyly, that Jack ventured to lay his heart at her feet.

And so the miller's son married the King's daughter, and there were great rejoicings throughout the land.

TOM THUMB

A long time ago a poor ploughman sat one evening by his fireside and poked the fire, while his wife sat opposite spinning. He said, "What a sad thing it is that we have no children, our home is so quiet, while other folks' houses are noisy and cheerful."

"Yes," answered his wife, and she sighed. "Even if it were an only one, and if it were no bigger than my thumb, I should be quite content."

Indeed, some time after this she had a little boy who was strong and healthy, but who was no bigger

than her thumb, and because of his tiny size they called him Tom Thumb.

One day Tom's mother was making a batter pudding, and that he might see how she mixed it, he climbed upon the edge of the bowl. But his foot slipped, he fell over head and ears into the batter, and his mother not observing him, stirred him into the pudding and popped him into the pot to boil.

Tom soon grew hotter and hotter, until he could not bear it any longer, and began to jump up and down. When Tom's mother saw the pudding behave in such a strange way she thought it was bewitched; and a tramp coming by just at the time, she handed it to him.

As soon as Tom got the batter out of his mouth, he began to cry aloud, which frightened the tramp so much that he flung the pudding over the hedge and ran as fast as he could run. The pudding being broken to pieces by the fall, Tom was released and walked home to his mother, who gave him a kiss and put him to bed.

Another morning Tom's mother

took him out with her when she went to milk the cow. It was a windy day, and to make sure that her little boy should not be blown away, she tied him by a silk thread to a thistle until she should milk the cow.

The cow, who was very fond of thistles, took Tom and the thistle up at one mouthful. While the cow chewed the thistle, Tom was terrified at her g r e a t t e e t h, which seemed ready to crush him to pieces, and roared, "Mother, Mother!"

"Where are you, Tommy?" said the mother.

"Here, mother! Here in the red cow's mouth!"

The mother was very excited, and the cow, surprised at such noises in her throat, opened her mouth and let Tom drop out. His mother picked him up and put him in her apron pocket.

When they reached home Tom explained that the cow thought the thistle a tempting morsel, and crunched it at a mouthful and swallowed it at a gulp. But Tom had not been bitten.

Another time Tom's father made him a whip of barley straw to drive the cattle with, and being one day in the field he slipped into a deep furrow. A crow flying over swooped down, and picked him up with a grain of corn, and flew with him to the top of a giant's castle by the seaside, where he left him. The giant coming soon after to walk on the terrace, picked him up and put him in his mouth, meaning to eat him. But Tom tickled his tongue so that the giant was glad to take him out of his mouth and throw him into the sea. A large fish then swallowed him. The fish was soon after caught and bought for the table of King Arthur. When it was cut open, everybody was delighted with Little Tom Thumb. The King liked Tom very much, and made him his dwarf, and he became the favorite of the whole court.

The King, when he rode on horseback, frequently took Tom in his hand; and if a shower of rain came on Tom used to creep into his Majesty's waistcoat pocket and sleep till the rain was over.

The King one day asked Tom about his father and mother, and when Tom informed him they were very poor people, the King led him into his treasury and told him he should pay his parents a visit and take with him as much money as he could carry. Tom procured a little purse, and putting a threepenny piece into it, with much labor and difficulty got it upon his back, and after traveling two days and nights arrived at his father's house.

How delighted Tom's father and mother were to see him, especially when he brought such an amazing sum of money with him. They placed him in a walnut shell by the fireside and gave him a hazel nut to eat. Now a hazel nut should have lasted Tom for a week, but he ate it all in that one day, and was ill.

The golden-haired Queen of Fairyland had always been interested in Tom, and when she knew that he was ill she came in a chariot drawn by winged mice and took Tom away with her to make him well.

He had been dressed in a velvet suit, lined with satin. When, after restoring him to health, the Queen summoned a great wind and placing Tom before it blew him to the court of King Arthur. Just at the time he should have landed in the courtyard of the palace the cook passed along with the King's bowl of hot milk, and poor Tom Thumb fell plump into the middle of it, and splash into the cook's eyes. Down went the bowl.

"Murder! murder!" screamed the cook. The cook was a red-faced, cross fellow, and swore to the King that Tom had done it out of mischief. So Tom was taken up, tried and sentenced to be beheaded.

When the little fellow heard this he was terrified, and with one spring jumped down the throat of the miller who stood by. Tom being lost, the court broke up, and away went the miller to his mill. But Tom did not leave him long at rest, but began to roll and tumble about so that the miller soon had to have a doctor.

When the doctor came Tom began to dance and sing, and the doctor was as much frightened as the miller was. He sent in great haste for six more doctors. While all these were considering what they should do, the miller happened to yawn and Tom gave a jump and landed on his feet in the middle of the table, and turned around and made a low bow to each.

The miller was very angry indeed. He caught Tom and threw him out the window into the river. A large salmon swimming by snapped him up at once. The salmon was caught that same day by one of the lords of the palace, who sent it as a present to the King, who ordered it to be cooked immediately. While the cook was preparing the salmon, he found poor Tom and ran with him directly to the King. The King, being busy with state affairs, said that he might be brought another day, so the cook put him into a mouse trap to keep him safe, and there he stayed for some time.

The King sent for Tom and forgave him for upsetting the milk, and ordered him new clothes and knighted him. The clothes were made of butterfly wings, and with a needle for a sword and a mouse for a steed, Tom went a-hunting.

As they rode by a farmhouse a cat came behind a door and would have gobbled the mouse up only for Tom, who drew his sword and pierced the cat, which made her leave go. Poor Tom was badly scratched and his clothes were torn by the cat's claws, and he was carried to the palace and laid in a little bed of down.

When Tom was well again the

King ordered a tiny gold palace to be made for him, a tiny chair and a tiny coach driven by six mice.

This made the Queen very angry, because she did not have a new coach. Therefore she decided to ruin him. She complained to the King that Tom had been very rude to her. The King was very angry and sent for Tom. To escape his fury he crept into an empty shell and there he lay until he was almost starved. At last one bright morning a beautiful butterfly settled on the ground near him. He crept out of the shell and climbed on to the butterfly's back.

The butterfly flew from field to field and from tree to tree and at last returned to the King's court. There the whole court tried to catch him, but could not, until at length Tom slipped from his back and fell into a watering-pot, in which he was almost drowned.

The Queen vowed his head should be cut off, and while they were getting ready to do it, he was secured once more in the mouse trap; when the cat seeing something stir, and supposing it to be a mouse, patted the trap about till she broke it and set Tom at liberty.

Afterwards the King, who missed

his favorite, pardoned him again, but Tom did not live very long to enjoy the King's favor. He was always ready to help others in distress, and one day, after undertaking to rescue a blue bottlefly from a spider's web, the spider attacked him so fiercely that he was overcome and fell down dead.

The King and his knights mourned for him for a long time, and were only consoled by erecting a beautiful monument, on which were recorded all the wonderful rescues and brave deeds of Tom Thumb.

JACK AND THE BEAN-STALK

In the days of King Alfred, there lived a poor woman, in a country village in England. She had been a widow some years, and had an only son named Jack, to whom she granted every wish. The result of this was that Jack did not pay attention to anything she said, but was idle, careless, and wasteful. His follies were not owing to a bad disposition, but to the fact that his mother had never checked him.

The poor woman one day met Jack with tears in her eyes, and for the first time in her life she could not help scolding him, saying, "You have at last brought me to ruin. I have not money enough to buy even a bit of bread for another day. Nothing now remains to sell but my poor cow. It grieves me sadly, but we must not starve!"

For a while Jack felt sorry, but this feeling soon passed away, and he begged his mother to let him sell the cow at the next village, and at last she gave her consent. As he was going along he met a butcher, who inquired why he was driving the cow from home. Jack replied

calling to his mother before he reached home, thinking to surprise her.

When she saw the beans and heard Jack's story, her patience quite left her. She was so angry that she threw the beans out of the window, and they were scattered in all directions, falling into the garden. Then she threw her apron over her head and cried bitterly. Not having anything to eat, they went supperless to bed.

Jack awoke early in the morning, and seeing something darkening the window, ran downstairs into the garden. Here he found that the beans had taken root, and had sprung up in a wonderful manner. The stalks were very thick, and had so twined together that they formed a ladder like a chain. Looking up he could not see the top, it appeared to be lost in the clouds.

He quickly made up his mind to climb to the top, and ran to tell his mother what he meant to do. She begged him not to go, but all in vain, for Jack set out, and after climbing for some hours reached the top, tired and quite worn out. Looking around he found himself in a strange country; not a tree,

that he was going to sell it. Now the butcher had some curious beans in his hat. They were of various colors and attracted Jack's attention. This the butcher noticed, and, knowing Jack's easy temper, thought this was the time to take advantage of it; so he asked what was the price of the cow, offering at the same time all the beans in his hat for her.

The silly boy could not hide the joy he felt at what he supposed was so good an offer, and the bargain was struck at once. The cow was thus exchanged for a few paltry beans. Jack made his way back, shrub, house, or living creature was to be seen.

Jack seated himself sadly upon a block of stone and thought of his mother, and after a while began to fear that he must die of hunger. Presently he saw in the distance an old woman.

While Jack was looking at her with the greatest surprise, she came up to him, and with a smile asked how he came there. Jack told her all about the bean-stalk. She asked him if he remembered his father. He replied that he did not; and added, that when he asked his mother about his father, she always would weep and tell him nothing.

The old woman replied: "I will tell you the story. But, before I begin, I require a promise to do what I tell you. I am a fairy, and you must do exactly what I desire, or you will be destroyed."

Jack promised to do exactly as she bade him, and the fairy then said:—

"Your father was a rich man. He was very good to the poor and always helped them. He made it a rule never to let a day pass without doing good to some one. His servants were all happy, and greatly loved their master and mistress. Now a giant lived a great many miles off, and he was as wicked as your father was good.

"He was poor, and wished to get rich no matter how. Hearing of

with a glass the coast could be seen clearly. One day the giant was using the telescope. The wind was very high, and he saw a fleet of ships in distress off the rock. He hastened to your father, and eagerly begged him to send all the servants he could spare to help the sufferers.

"Every one was at once sent off. The giant then joined your father in the study, who gave him a favorite book, when the giant killed him.

"You were then three months old. Your mother went into the study, and how shocked she was on finding your father dead! The giant found her, and was about to serve her and you as he had done your father, but she fell at his feet, and begged him to spare your life and hers.

"Remorse, for a moment, seemed to touch his heart. He granted your lives, but first he made her take a solemn oath never to tell you who your father was, or to answer any questions about him, assuring her that if she did he would put both of you to death.

"Your mother took you in her arms and fled as quickly as possible. She was scarcely gone when

your father, he thought it would be a good thing to make friends with him. He moved into your neighborhood, where he pretended that he was a gentleman who had just lost all he had by an earthquake.

"Your father believed his story, and gave him rooms in his own house, and caused him and his wife to be treated like visitors of importance.

"Things went on in this way for some time, the giant becoming more impatient to carry out his plan. At last his chance came. Your father's house was at some distance from the seashore, but

Jack set out, and after climbing for some hours, reached the top.

the giant repented that he had allowed her to escape. He would
have pursued her instantly, but he
had to look out for his own safety,
as it was necessary he should be
gone before the servants returned.
Therefore, he loaded himself and
his wife with money and jewels, set
the house on fire in several places,
and when the servants came back
the house was burned to the
ground.

"I became your father's guardian
at his birth; but a short time before
the giant went to your father's
house, I did something wrong; to

punish me my power was taken
away for a time—so it prevented my
helping him.

"The day on which you met the
butcher, my power was given me
again. It was I who made you take
the beans in exchange for the cow.
By my power the bean-stalk grew
so tall and became a ladder.

"Now, the giant lives in this
country, and you are the person to
punish him. You will have dan-
gers, but you must avenge the
death of your father. As to the
giant's possessions, you may seize
all you can; because they belonged

to your father. One thing I desire, do not let your mother know you have heard your father's history till you see me again.

"Go along this road until you come to the castle where the giant lives. I will protect and guard you."

When the fairy had ended she disappeared, leaving Jack to pursue his journey. He walked on till after sunset, when, to his great joy, he saw a large castle.

A woman was at the door; he spoke to her and begged her to give him a morsel of bread and a night's lodging.

She expressed the greatest surprise at seeing him, for it was well known that her husband was a very powerful giant, and that he would never eat anything but human flesh if he could possibly get it.

This account greatly terrified Jack, but still he hoped to escape from the giant; and again begged the woman to take him in for one night only, and hide him where she thought he would be safe. The good woman at last agreed, for she was of a kindly nature, and took him into the house.

They entered a fine great hall, then passed through a long gallery; it was very dark—just light enough to show that instead of a wall on one side, there was a grating of iron, which parted off a dungeon, from whence issued the moans of those poor victims whom the cruel giant kept in confinement.

At the farther end of the long gallery there was a very large kitchen, and a fire was burning in the grate. The good woman told Jack to sit down, and gave him plenty to eat and drink. Jack, not seeing anything here to frighten him, soon forgot his fear, and was just begin-

ning to enjoy himself when he was aroused by a loud knocking at the door, which made the whole house shake. The giant's wife ran to hide him in the oven, and then went to let her husband in. Jack heard him say in a voice like thunder, "Wife, I smell fresh meat."

"Oh! my dear," replied she, "it is nothing but the people in the dungeon."

The giant appeared to believe her, and walked into the very kitchen where poor Jack was hidden, who was more frightened than ever.

At last the giant seated himself by the fireside, while his wife made the supper. Little by little Jack got over his fright so far as to look at the giant through a small crack, and he was quite astonished to see what an enormous quantity he ate.

When supper was over the giant told his wife to bring him his hen. A very beautiful hen was then brought and placed on the table before him.

Jack's desire to see what would happen was very great, and soon he saw that every time the giant said "Lay!" the hen laid an egg of solid gold. At length the giant fell asleep by the fireside and snored like the roaring of a cannon.

After a time, Jack, finding the giant still asleep, and not likely to awaken soon, crept softly out of his hiding-place, seized the hen, and ran off with her. He easily found the way to the bean-stalk, and got down it better and quicker than he expected.

He found his mother crying bitterly, for she was certain he had come to some sad end through his rashness. Jack showed his hen, and told his mother how valuable it was.

"And now, mother," said Jack, "I have brought home that which

will quickly make us rich; and I hope to make up for the sorrow I have caused you through my idleness."

The hen laid as many golden eggs as they wished; they sold them, and in a little time they had as much riches as they needed.

For some months Jack and his mother lived very happily together; but he remembered the fairy's commands, and longed to climb the bean-stalk and pay the giant another visit, in order to carry away some more of his treasures.

Jack thought of his journey again and again, but still he could not make up his mind to speak of it to his mother, being quite sure that she would try to prevent his going.

However, one day he told her that he must take a journey up the bean-stalk. She begged him not to think of it, and tried all in her power to keep him from doing so.

Jack, finding that all he said was useless, pretended to give it up, though he made up his mind to go at all events. So he had a dress made which would disguise

him, and found something to color his skin in such a way that he thought no one would know him again.

A few mornings after this, he arose very early, colored the skin of his face, and climbed the beanstalk a second time. He was very tired when he reached the top, and very hungry. But after resting some time, he went on his way to the giant's castle. He reached it late in the evening, and found the woman at the door as before. Jack told her a pitiful tale, and begged her to give him some food and a night's lodging.

She told him that one night she took into her house a poor, hungry boy, who was half dead from travelling; but the ungrateful fellow had stolen one of the giant's treasures, and ever since that her husband had been worse than before, continually scolding her for being the cause of his loss.

Jack at once knew that he was listening to a story in which he was the chief actor; he did his best to persuade the good woman to take him in, but he found it a very hard task.

At last she consented; and as she led the way Jack saw that everything was just as it was before. She took him into the kitchen, and after he had done eating and drinking, she hid him in an old closet. The giant returned at the usual time, and walked in so heavily that the house shook.

He seated himself by the fire and soon after said, "Wife, I smell fresh meat!"

The wife replied it was the crows, who had brought a piece of raw meat and left it on the roof.

The giant at last having eaten till he was quite satisfied, said to his wife, "I must have something to amuse me: either my bags of money or my harp."

He told her to bring down his bags of gold and silver. Jack, as before, peeped out of his hiding-place, and presently the giant's wife brought two very large bags into the room. One was filled with gold and the other with silver pieces. They were both placed before the giant, who began scolding his poor wife for being so long away.

The giant took his bags, and began to count the money. First, the bag which contained the silver was emptied, and the contents placed upon the table. Jack saw the glittering heaps, and wished they were his own.

The giant (little thinking he was so closely watched) counted the silver over several times; and then put it into the bag again.

The other bag was opened next, and the golden pieces placed upon the table.

When the giant had counted over the gold till he was tired, he put it up more securely if possible than he had put up the silver before. Then he leaned back on his chair by the fireside and fell asleep. He snored so loud that Jack compared his noise to the roaring of the sea.

At last Jack, feeling sure the giant was asleep, stole out of his hiding-place and went near him, seized the bags, and throwing them over his shoulders ran out of the kitchen. He reached the door in safety and found it was daylight. On his way to the top of the bean-stalk he found it hard work to carry the heavy money-bags.

Jack was delighted when he found himself near the bean-stalk. When he reached it he soon went to the bottom, and at once ran to seek his mother. To his great surprise there was no one in the cottage.

An old woman at last directed him to a house near by, where he found his mother ill. But on being told of her son's safe return, his mother began to improve and at last became quite well again. Jack at once gave her his two valuable bags, and with the money the cottage was rebuilt and well furnished and they lived happily for a long time after.

For three years Jack said no more of the bean-stalk, but he could not forget it, although he would not mention it for he feared to make his mother unhappy. She, too, would not speak of the bean-stalk, lest it should remind her son to make another journey.

In spite of the comforts Jack enjoyed at home, he often thought about the bean-stalk; and it prevented him from being happy.

The idea grew upon him so that he could think of nothing else. His mother saw that something lay heavy upon his mind, and tried to discover the cause; but Jack knew what the consequence would be, should she succeed.

Finding, however, that his desire grew too strong for him, he began to make secret plans for his journey; and, on the longest day of the year, he arose as soon as it was light and climbed the bean-stalk, reaching the top with some little trouble. He found the journey much as it was on the two former times. He arrived at the giant's castle in the evening, and found his wife standing, as usual, at the door. Jack had disguised himself so completely that she did not appear to have the least recollection of him. However, when he told her of his hunger and poverty, in order to be allowed to enter the castle, he found it very difficult indeed to persuade her. At last he succeeded, and was hidden in a large copper kettle this time.

When the giant returned, he said, "Wife, I smell fresh meat."

But Jack felt quite easy in his mind, as the giant had said so before, and had been soon satisfied. However, the giant started up all at once, and his wife could not prevent him from searching all round the room.

While this was going on, Jack was very frightened, and wished he was at home. When the giant came near the kettle and put his hand upon the lid, Jack thought his death was certain. The giant ended his search there, though, without moving the lid, and seated himself by the fireside. Jack was so frightened he was afraid to move or even to breathe, lest he should be discovered. The giant at last ate a hearty supper, and when he had finished he commanded his wife to bring his harp.

Jack peeped under the lid, and saw the most beautiful harp that could be thought of; it was placed on the table by the giant, who said, "Play!" and it instantly played of its own accord without being touched. The music was the sweetest Jack had ever heard.

Jack felt more anxious to get the

harp than either of the former treasures; fortunately for him the music soon lulled the giant into a sound sleep. Now, was the time to carry off the harp.

Jack got out of the kettle, and seized the harp. But the harp, being enchanted by a fairy, called out loudly, "Master! master!"

The giant awoke, and tried to run after Jack; but he had eaten so much that he could hardly stand.

Poor Jack ran as fast as he could, and in a little time the giant recovered enough to walk slowly, or rather to stagger after him. But Jack was the first at the top of the bean-stalk. The giant called after him in a voice like thunder.

The moment Jack got down the bean-stalk he ran for a hatchet.

Now, just at that instant, the giant was beginning to descend; but Jack cut the bean-stalk close off at the roots, which made the giant fall headlong into the garden. The fall was so great that it killed him, thereby releasing the world from a dangerous enemy.

At this instant the fairy appeared, and first spoke to Jack's mother, explaining everything relating to the journeys up the bean-stalk.

The fairy told Jack to be dutiful to his mother, and to follow his father's good example, which was the only way to be happy. She then disappeared.

Jack heartily begged his mother's pardon for all the sorrow he had caused her, promising to be very dutiful and obedient to her in the future.

DEAR LITTLE FRIEND:

If you have enjoyed this book ask your bookseller for the other volumes of THE POPULAR STORY SERIES, edited by Watty Piper. They are:

CHILDREN OF MANY LANDS

MOTHER GOOSE RHYMES

NURSERY TALES CHILDREN LOVE

FOLK TALES CHILDREN LOVE

ANIMAL FRIENDS STORY BOOK

THE PLATT & MUNK CO., INC.

LIST OF BOOKS

Edited by WATTY PIPER

ANIMAL FRIENDS STORY BOOK
THE BRIMFUL BOOK
THE GATEWAY TO STORYLAND
MOTHER GOOSE RHYMES AND NURSERY TALES
FAIRY TALES THAT NEVER GROW OLD
CHILDREN'S HOUR WITH BONNIE AND BUNNY
CHILDREN'S HOUR WITH MR. TABBY CAT
CHILDREN'S HOUR WITH THE BIRDS
FAMOUS FAIRY TALES
FAMOUS RHYMES MOTHER GOOSE
THE ROAD IN STORYLAND
LITTLE BLACK SAMBO AND OTHER STORIES
THE GINGERBREAD BOY AND OTHER STORIES

THE STAR BOOKS FOR CHILDREN

HAPPINESS
ON
EVERY
PAGE

TRADE MARK
THE PLATT & MUNK CO.